S0-AXJ-693

SNOW BEAST COMES TO PLAY

What?!?

PHIL GOSIER

SCHOLASTIC INC.

For Mom

No part of this publication may be reproduced, stored in a retrieval system, or transmitted in any form or by any means, electronic, mechanical, photocopying, recording, or otherwise, without written permission of the publisher. For information regarding permission, write to Roaring Brook Press, a division of Holtzbrinck Publishing Holdings Limited Partnership, 175 Fifth Avenue, New York, NY 10010.

ISBN 978-1-338-45699-8

Copyright © 2017 by Phil Gosier. All rights reserved. Published by Scholastic Inc., 557 Broadway, New York, NY 10012, by arrangement with Roaring Brook Press, a division of Holtzbrinck Publishing Holdings Limited Partnership. SCHOLASTIC and associated logos are trademarks and/or registered trademarks of Scholastic Inc.

The publisher does not have any control over and does not assume any responsibility for author or third-party websites or their content.

12 11 10 9 8 7 6 5 4 3 2 1   19 20 21 22 23 24

Printed in the U.S.A.   40

First Scholastic printing, January 2019

Book design by Andrew Arnold

Snow is Penny's favorite thing.

Snow!

She likes to sing to it.

Snow, snowy snow!

She loves to stomp in it.

Snow! Snowy! Snow!

She knows not to walk under icicles.

Careful!

And most of all, she knows to watch out for snow beasts.

Have **YOU** ever met a snow beast?

Snow beasts only come out in the snow. They
have enormous heads, gigantic bellies, and great big feet.

Some like to nap.
SNOOORE!

Some complain it's cold!
BRRR-R-R!

And some wonder why they have bigger feet than everyone else. **HMM.**

But this snow beast was different.

This snow beast didn't want to nap.

He wasn't cold.

And he didn't want to compare feet.

This beast wanted to **PLAY**!

So he decided to do something
snow beasts almost never do.

He decided to make a friend.

Snow Beast never had a friend before. But he knew
friendships should always start with "Hello."

He knew that for sure.

Unfortunately, snow beasts can be very LOUD.

He saw a man moving snow . . .

Snow Beast knew
friends should always
help one another.

WANT TO HELP!

WAAAUUGH!

Unfortunately, snow beasts
are shockingly large.

He knew it was important
to try to join in!

SNOW BEAST SORRY!!

MOMMY! MOMMY!

Unfortunately, snow beasts
are a little clumsy.

Snow Beast had tried his
best . . . but nothing worked.

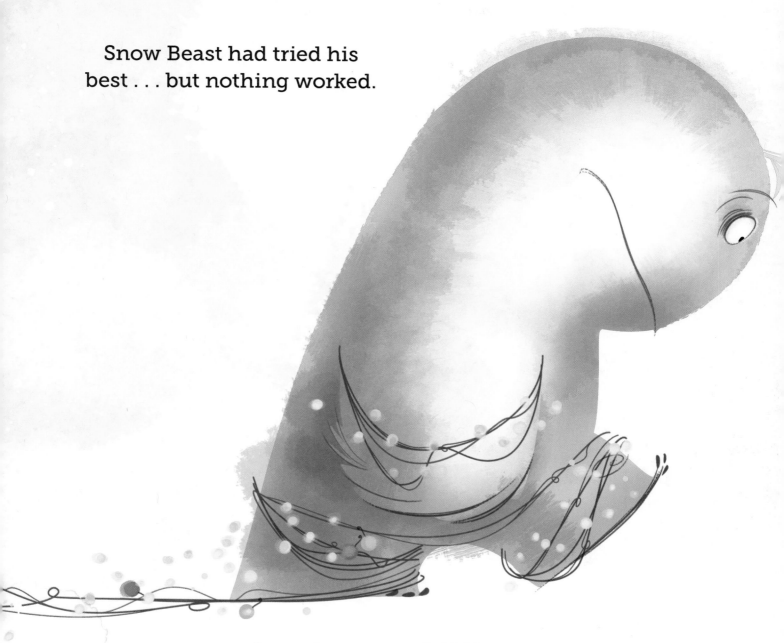

Snow beasts are **LOUD**.
And **LARGE**.
And more than a little **CLUMSY**.

But when they're sad, they're just like you and me.

They cry.

ALL FRIENDS RUN AWAY!

He only wants to play!

I still think we should RUN!

Penny imagined how she would feel
if no one wanted to play with her.

So she decided to do something
nobody else had done.

She made friends.